W9-BFG-201

BARBARA PARK

Junie B., First Grader
Dumb Bunny

illustrated by Denise Brunkus

SCHOLASTIC INC.
New York Toronto London Auckland Sydney
Mexico City New Delhi Hong Kong Buenos Aires

Dear my brand-newest friend Makenzie Moore,
This book is dedicated especially to you from me!
I hope it makes you laugh and laugh!
                                        Love and hugs,
                                   Junie B., First Grader
P.S. Plus also, thank you to Make-A-Wish for introducing us!

ISBN-13: 978-0-545-15452-9
ISBN-10: 0-545-15452-9

Copyright © 2007 by Barbara Park. Illustrations copyright © 2007 by Denise Brunkus. All rights reserved. Published by Scholastic Inc., 557 Broadway, New York, NY 10012, by arrangement with Random House Children's Books, a division of Random House, Inc. JUNIE B., FIRST GRADER® stylized design is a registered trademark of Barbara Park, used under license. SCHOLASTIC and associated logos are trademarks and/or registered trademarks of Scholastic Inc.

12 11 10 9 8 7 6 5 4 3 2 1   9 10 11 12 13 14/0

Printed in the U.S.A.   40

This edition first printing, January 2009

Contents

1

Dumb Bunnies
and Clucks

Monday

Dear first-grade journal,

Dumb bunny!

Dumb bunny!

Dumb bunny!

I am not allowed to say dumb
bunny! On account of my
teacher heard ~~herd~~ me call May that
name on the playground. And

he said for me to knock it off.

Only here is something I just thought of.

Even if I can't say dumb bunny out loud, I can still think it inside my head. 'Cause heads are silent. Which is what I like about heads.

I am going to try it out right now.

I put down my pencil and looked at May.

Then I squinted my eyes real teensy.

And I thought that name to just myself.

Dumb bunny! Dumb bunny! Dumb bunny! Dumb bunny!

May looked suspicious at me.

"What are you doing, Junie Jones? Why are you squinting like that?" she asked. "Stop it right now. Stop that squinting."

I paused my squint.

"I'm not just *squinting* at you, May. I'm also thinking a name about you inside my head. But you don't even know what name I'm thinking. 'Cause heads are silent. Which is what I like about heads," I said.

May frowned.

I started my squint again.

Dumb bunny, dumb bunny, dumb bunny, dumb bunny, dumb bunny, I thought.

After I finished, I brushed my hands together very satisfied.

"There. That ought to hold me for a while," I said.

May kept on frowning.

Then *BLAM!*

She exploded out of her chair! And she zoomed to the front of the room!

"Mr. Scary! Mr. Scary! Junie B. called me that name again! I *know* she did! Only she thought it inside her head! And that is just plain sneaky!"

Mr. Scary was writing at his desk.

He closed his eyes and did a big breath.

"May, what are our three new rules about tattling?" he asked. "You and I came up with three new rules to control your tattling, remember? Can you tell me what they are, please?"

May stood there a real long time.

She did not like the three new rules, I believe.

Finally, she started to say them.

"Rule number one: Count to twenty before I tattle," she grumped.

Mr. Scary nodded. "Yes, May. Excellent. That's the first rule. Go on."

"Rule number two," said May. "If I still feel like tattling, count to twenty *again*."

Mr. Scary did a thumbs-up.

"Yes, good . . . and rule number three?"

May sucked in her cheeks.

"Rule number three: If I *still* feel like tattling after that . . . go home . . . eat dinner . . . go to bed . . . wake up . . . eat breakfast . . . come back to school . . . raise my hand to tattle . . . then put my hand over my mouth . . . and please be quiet," she said.

Mr. Scary clapped his happy hands.

"Perfect! You've got it! Those are *exactly* the rules we talked about, aren't they?" he said. "I'm very proud of you for remembering them!"

He stood up and walked her back to her chair.

"You have a *great* memory for rules, May," he said. "But the next step is to actually *follow* the rules, okay? And I don't believe you counted to twenty this time, did you?"

I leaned over and tapped on him.

"I can vouch for that," I said. "There was definitely no counting."

Mr. Scary frowned at me.

"I'll deal with you in a minute, Miss Jones," he said. "You and I are going to review the rules on name-calling."

I did a gulp.

"But I didn't even *call* her a name, Mr. Scary. All I did was think a name in my head," I said.

May flashed her angry eyes.

"No, you did not just *think* it, Junie Jones. You *told* me you were thinking it. And that is exactly like saying it, almost," she said.

She went on.

"Plus you didn't even think it *quietly*. You thought it so loud that I could hear it in your brain."

May looked up at Mr. Scary.

"My ears were tested last year in kindergarten," she said. "The nurse said I can hear as good as a North American barn owl."

Mr. Scary stared at her a real long time.

"No, May. No. I'm sorry," he said finally. "But the nurse did *not* tell you that. You do *not* hear as well as a North American barn owl."

May squirmed in her chair a little bit.

Squirming is what happens after fibbing.

At least that has always been my experience.

After a minute, May put her head on her desk. And she covered up with her sweater.

Mr. Scary bent down next to me.

"And as for you, Miss Jones . . . this is the absolute last time that I *ever* want to talk to you about name-calling," he said. "I don't want you to *say* dumb bunny, or *think* dumb bunny, or *sing* dumb bunny, or *hum* dumb bunny, or *write* dumb bunny. Do you understand?"

I tapped my fingers on my desk.

"But then what am I supposed to do when May is mean to me?" I asked him. "I have to call her *something* or else she won't even know I'm mad."

I thought for a second. Then I clapped my hands together.

"Hey! I know! Maybe I could just *think* the *dumb* part in my head. And I'll call her just plain *bunny*!" I said. "Would just plain *bunny* be okay with you?"

May popped up from under her sweater.

"No, no, no!" she grouched. "Just plain *bunny* isn't nice, either!"

My friend named Sheldon stood up.

"*Bunny* isn't nice? How come *bunny* isn't nice?" he asked. "I have an aunt named Bunny. And she's very, *very* nice."

Sheldon looked at Mr. Scary.

"My aunt Bunny is married to my uncle Vern," he said. "Aunt Bunny has a lot of—"

Mr. Scary quick held up his hand.

"Yes, Sheldon, we *know*. You've told us many interesting things about your aunt Bunny. But right now we don't need to hear any more about your aunt Bunny's—"

"Skull tattoos," said Sheldon.

"Please sit down," said Mr. Scary.

Across the room, Lucille sprang right up.

"Well, I love, love, *love* bunnies!" she said. "And so this subject is perfect timing for me! Because I'm having a big party at my giant house on Saturday! And *all* of you are invited to come!"

She bounced up and down real excited.

"And guess what else? A very famous bunny is going to be there to meet you! Guess who it is, everyone! Guess the bunny! Guess the bunny!" she said.

Room One thought real hard.

Then all of us started to guess at once.

"Bugs Bunny?"

"Buster Bunny?"

"The Bionic Bunny?"

"Thumper?" we guessed.

10

Lucille rolled her eyes.

"No, no, no," she said. "My bunny is *way* more famous than those dumb cartoon guys."

We guessed some more.

"The Trix Rabbit?"

"The Velveteen Rabbit?"

"Peter Rabbit?" we asked.

Lucille stamped her foot.

"NO!" she said again. "What's *wrong* with you people? It's the *Easter Bunny*! Haven't you ever heard of the Easter Bunny?"

She reached into her desk and pulled out some fancy envelopes.

Then she waved them around real angry.

"Do you see these invitations? Huh? Do you?" she asked. "These are invitations to an Easter-egg hunt at my rich, expensive

house! And I was going to pass them out at lunch. But if you dumb clucks never even *heard* of the Easter Bunny, just never mind the whole thing!"

After that, she did a huffy. And she flounced back in her chair.

Mr. Scary hurried over there.

Then he quick got her up.

And he took her by the hand.

And he walked her into the hall.

They were gone a real long time.

When they finally came back, Lucille said she is sorry for calling us *dumb clucks*.

That is some kind of insult, apparently.

Then she took the envelopes out of her desk again. And she gave everyone an invitation.

And so, yippee, yippee!

Hurray, hurray!

Room One is going to a party!

2
■ ■ ■ ■ ■ ■ ■ ■ ■ ■
Clothes and Nubs

Lucille was still mad at lunch.

"I just don't *get* it," she grouched. "How could anyone forget the Easter Bunny? The Easter Bunny brings candy right to your door."

Lennie did a frown at her.

"He doesn't bring candy to *my* door, Lucille," he said. "The Easter Bunny is a different religion than me. I'm Jewish."

Shirley nodded.

"I'm Jewish, too, Lucille," she said. "I've never even *been* to an Easter-egg hunt before. What do you wear to something like that, anyway?"

Lucille stood up and fluffed herself.

"Well—since the Easter Bunny and I are the *same* religion—*I'm* going to wear a fancy Easter dress, Shirley," she said.

Shirley thought for a minute. Then she nodded.

"Hmm. Then I guess I will wear a fancy Jewish dress," she said.

Lennie's eyes lighted up.

"Really, Shirley? You mean we have our own clothing line?" he asked.

He smiled.

"Then I think I will wear some fancy Jewish pants," he said.

My friend named Herbert tapped on his chin.

"Let's see. Since *I'm* a Pressed-byterian,

I guess I should wear Pressed-byterian pants," he said.

He turned and looked at me.

"*Pressed-byterian* means we iron out our wrinkles, I think," he said.

Just then, Sheldon slapped the table with his hand.

"Hey, *I* know! I will wear a fancy turban! A fancy turban is religious clothes, right?" he asked. "I love fancy turbans!"

Mr. Scary was listening to us while he ate.

He quick put down his sandwich.

"Boys and girls, you're getting *way* off track here," he said. "Lucille's Easter-egg hunt is *not* a religious party. *Really.* I've spoken to her mother about it. It's more of a spring picnic with an egg-hunt activity. Am I right, Lucille?"

"Yes," she said. "My mother said the Easter Bunny isn't even working that day. He's just going to hop around the party . . . and smile . . . and have his picture taken with people."

I thought about that for a second.

"I don't think bunnies should smile," I said. "Bunnies have yellow teeth, like clown teeth. Except bunny teeth are way pointier."

Sheldon nodded.

"My aunt Bunny has a pointy tooth," he said. "She can stab a pickle with it. And the pickle just stays there."

All of us stared at him.

Sheldon has the interestingest family I ever heard of.

Lucille did a big breath.

"Well, I don't care about pointy bunny

teeth," she said. "Bunnies have cute floppy ears, and puffy, fluffy tails, and itchy, twitchy little noses."

I kept on picturing their teeth. "Bunny teeth can nibble your head into a nub," I said.

"No, they can*not,* Junie B. Jones," she said back.

"Oh yes they can, Lucille whatever-your-last-name-is," I said. "I saw it on *Oprah*."

Mr. Scary glared at me.

I ducked down in my seat. And I quieted my voice.

"*Oprah* has a lot of nub information," I said very soft.

Mr. Scary glared again.

I started to squirm.

Teachers can spot a fib a mile away.

* * *

At recess, Lucille told us more about the party.

She said that there was going to be lots of delicious food to eat. Plus also, there was going to be an exciting prize for the Easter-egg winner.

"And wait till you hear *this*!" she said. "My daddy is going to hide a real pretend *golden egg*! And whoever finds the golden egg will win The Grand Prize of the Day! And *that* is a fabulous playdate with . . . ME! LUCILLE!"

She twirled around and hugged herself.

"And it's not just any old fabulous play-date with me, either!" she said. "The winner is going to get to go swimming with me in my *heated* indoor swimming pool that we just had enclosed!"

She did a little shiver and rubbed her arms.

"Isn't that exciting, everyone?" she asked. "Doesn't that give you the *tinkles*?"

She looked around.

"Well? Doesn't it? Huh? Doesn't it make you tinkle all over?" she asked.

All of the children looked curious at each other.

Herbert rocked back and forth on his feet a minute.

"Um, I think you mean the *tingles*," he said at last.

José nodded. "Sí, Lucille. You definitely mean the *tingles*," he said.

Lucille squinted at those two.

"Tingles . . . tinkles . . . *whatever*. The point is, a playdate with me gives you goose bumps on your arms," she said. "Just look at your arms, people. Don't you see them? Don't you see the goose bumps?"

All of us looked at our arms.

None of us saw the goose bumps.

We waited and waited real patient.

And then *finally*—

"GOOSE BUMPS!" shouted Sheldon. "I SEE GOOSE BUMPS, LUCILLE!"

He ran to her and pointed.

"Look, Lucille! See them? See my goose bumps?" he asked.

Lucille's face beamed very happy.

"Ooooh, Sheldon! Those are the goose-bumpiest goose bumps I ever saw! Thank you, Shelsie! Thank you for those goose bumps!" she said.

After that, she gave him a big hug. And she waved her fingers at us.

"Well, ta-ta, everyone," she said. "It's time for me to go look at myself in the cafeteria window."

Then she shook her shiny hair. And she skipped away.

Sheldon kept on standing there.

He was shocked from the hug, I think.

Then, all of a sudden, his whole face lighted up. And he began to shout.

"Lucille! Wait up! I'll look at myself in the cafeteria window, too!" he shouted.

He took off skipping after her.

I smiled to see that.

"I think Sheldon has a crunch on Lucille," I said to my friend Herbert.

Herb looked funny at me.

"You mean *crush*, Junie B. He has a *crush* on Lucille," he said.

I started to laugh.

"Don't be ridiculous, Herbert. It's definitely *crunch*," I said. "I am excellent at eggspressions."

Herb looked funny at me again.

I do not know why.

After a minute, Sheldon and Lucille
skipped past us.

They were smiling and giggling and chasing each other.

Sheldon was calling to her.

"Come back here, you springy little lamb!" he called.

I slapped my knee.

"Springy little lamb! Ha! He called her a springy little lamb! That is a hoot!" I said.

May heard me talking.

"It's not funny, Junie Jones. Can't you see what he's doing?" she said. "Sheldon is trying to get in good with Lucille so she'll tell him where the golden egg is hidden. He's just trying to win the playdate to swim in her pool."

She followed him with her eyes.

"He's not going to get away with it, though," she said.

After that, she cupped her hands around

her mouth. And she shouted after him.

"You can just forget about it, Sheldon Potts! *I'm* going to be the one who finds the golden egg! Not *you*! I've got eyes like a red-tailed hawk!"

I looked at her very curious.

May has a lot of bird parts, I believe.

Also, she is cuckoo.

And that is not name-calling.

That is just the truth.

3

■ ■ ■ ■ ■ ■ ■ ■ ■

Waiting and Waiting

On Saturday morning, I jumped out of bed very excited.

'Cause today was the day of the party, of course!

"The Easter-egg hunt! The Easter-egg hunt! Today is the day of the Easter-egg hunt!" I sang real loud.

I ran into Mother and Daddy's room. And I turned on their light.

"The Easter-egg hunt! The Easter-egg hunt! Today is the day of the Easter-egg hunt!" I sang again.

Mother opened one eyeball.

"It's not time to get up yet, Junie B.," she said. "It's still dark outside. Please go back to bed."

I put my head next to her face.

"Yeah, only I don't think that's actually possible," I said. "On account of my brain is already activated."

Mother put her pillow over her head.

I lifted it up.

"I'm going to find the golden egg today," I said. "I told you about that. Right, Mother? Whoever finds the golden egg gets to swim in Lucille's hot water."

I hugged myself very happy.

"I would love, love, *love* to swim in hot water," I said. "Except for Sheldon and May want that prize, too. Plus Lucille loves Sheldon. And so maybe she might give him a hint or something. And a hint would not be good."

I did a little frown.

"Plus here is another problem," I said. "May has bird parts. And birds can see as good as a hawk."

Mother pretended to snore.

I did a huffy breath at her.

Sometimes mothers do not act their old age.

Finally, I put the pillow back on her head. And I went back to my room.

Then I picked up my stuffed elephant named Philip Johnny Bob. And we skipped to my closet to pick out party clothes.

We looked at all my hangers.

"Hmm," I said. "Hmm, hmm, hmm. What kind of clothes are good egg-hunting clothes, do you think, Phil?"

Philip tapped on his trunk.

Well, let's see. Good egg-hunting clothes should be easy to run in, probably. 'Cause when you spot an egg, you will have to beat people to it. Right? he asked.

"Right," I said. "Plus good egg-hunting clothes should not be a dress, either. On account of sometimes—when I am beating people to an egg—I will have to tackle them and get in a scuffle."

Correct, said Philip. *Tackling and scuffling often happens in egg hunts.*

He thought some more.

Also, good egg-hunting clothes should have big pockets to carry all the eggs you're going to find, he said.

I nodded. "Yes. Plus good egg clothes have to be pretty. Right, Phil?" I said. "Because this *is* a fancy party, you know."

I know, said Phil. *Egg clothes should definitely be pretty . . . like . . . like . . .*

We looked some more.

Then ha! Both of us spotted the pretty clothes at once!

"LIKE THOSE BRAND-NEW LAVENDER OVERALLS THAT MOTHER JUST BOUGHT!" we shouted real joyful.

Phil threw himself way high in the air.

Yes! Yes! The brand-new lavender overalls will be perfect, Junie B.! 'Cause lavender is 'zactly like purple, almost! And purple is the color of your favorite glasses!

He flung himself in the air again.

We are a genius at picking egg clothes! he said.

"Yes! We *are* a genius, Philip!" I said back. "I cannot lose the egg hunt in this perfect outfit!"

After that, I quick put on my lavender overalls.

And then me and Philip ran to the window.

And we sat down on the floor.

And we waited and waited for daylight to come.

The party was supposed to start at lunchtime.

There was going to be a picnic before the egg hunt.

That information was printed right on Lucille's fancy invitation.

I read it to Mother and Daddy at breakfast.

"A picnic lunch will be served on the grounds before the event," I read.

I smiled.

"I enjoy eating on the ground," I said.

Mother laughed.

"Oh, I don't think you'll be eating on the *ground*, Junie B.," she said. "*Grounds* are what rich people call their lawns and gardens."

I got down from the table and looked outside.

"Do we have grounds?" I asked.

Mother rolled her eyes and looked at Daddy.

"Heavens no, Junie B.," she said. "What *we* have is weeds and crabgrass."

Daddy sucked in his cheeks at her.

Weeds and crabgrass is an *issue*, apparently.

After breakfast, I waited for it to be time to leave.

It was the longest morning I ever saw.

Then *finally, finally, finally!* Daddy said it was time to go. And so I ran to the car lickety-split!

Lickety-split is the grown-up word for zippedy fast.

It took forever to get to Lucille's house.

We drove and drove and drove.

Then whew! At last! We turned down Lucille's long driveway!

"Lucille's house! Lucille's house! We're finally at Lucille's house!" I shouted out.

I leaned my nose against the window.

"Remember when I came here last year, Daddy?" I said. "Me and my friend Grace spent the night at this place! And I ate dinner and breakfast with her rich, expensive nanna!"

Then . . . oh my gosh!

I *saw* her!

I saw the rich, expensive nanna!

She was standing there with Lucille's mother and daddy and brother. They were welcoming all the cars.

I opened my door and I ran to her.

"WELL, WELL, WELL! WE MEET AGAIN, NANNA!" I hollered real happy.

Then I hugged my arms around her middle. And I tried to lift her off the ground. Only she didn't actually budge that good.

I stepped back and looked at her.

The nanna had put on a few pounds, I believe.

After that I tried to lift her again. But this time, she took my arms away.

"Oh dear, no, young lady. You mustn't try to pick me up," she said. "You'll hurt yourself."

I looked at her kind of puzzled.

"Yeah, only I'm not a young lady, Nanna," I said. "Look! See? It's *me*! It's Junie B. Jones!"

I pointed at my face.

"Don't you remember me? Huh? I spent the night here with Lucille and Grace. Remember that, Nanna? It was the time of our life!" I said.

The nanna looked closer at me.

Then, all of a sudden, drops of sweaty came on her head.

She took out a tissue and dabbed herself.

"Oh my. Oh dear. Yes, I remember *now*," she said.

She did a little shiver.

"Junie B. Jones . . . I remember you *well*."

I skipped around her in a circle.

"Today is going to be fun, right, Nanna?

Today I am going to find the golden egg!"

After I skipped, I held out my hand to do a high five. But the nanna didn't actually respond. And so I just swatted at her sleeve, and that's all.

Just then, another car drove up in the driveway.

I turned around.

And oh boy, oh boy!

It was my good friend named Shirley!

Plus after Shirley came Sheldon! And after Sheldon came Roger! And after Roger came Camille and Chenille, and Herbert, and José, and Lennie.

And then all the rest of the children in Room One came, too!

Only wait till you hear this!

I didn't see *you-know-who*.

I looked all around to be sure.

Then I crossed my fingers for luck.

And I hoped that maybe May wouldn't show up at all. 'Cause maybe she would forget that the party was today, possibly.

I thought a minute.

Or else maybe her daddy's car would get four flat tires . . .

Or maybe his battery would go dead . . .

Or maybe his muffler would fall off in the middle of the street.

I thought some more and did a grin.

Or else *maaaaybe* May was playing in her backyard this morning. And she bent over to tie her shoe. And *FLOOF!* She got carried off by a North American barn owl!

I bent over and laughed out loud.

Now *that* was a good one!

4

■ ■ ■ ■ ■ ■ ■ ■ ■

Eggs and Sweaty
and Other Stuff

Just as I was getting hope . . . another car pulled up.

And phooey!

Sitting in the backseat was—

"MAY! MAY! MAY'S HERE!" she shouted through the open window.

She was clapping and cheering for herself.

Then she jumped out of the car.

And she ran to Lucille's family.

And she started shaking all their hands.

"Hello! Hello! I'm May! And I've come to win the golden egg!" she told them.

She skipped to Lucille and held out her dress.

"Look, Lucille! Look! Look! My dress is frilly just like yours!" she said. "I gave this outfit a lot of thought. 'Cause I wanted us to look like best friends today!"

She threw her arm around Lucille's shoulder.

Sheldon ran up and took it off.

"Whoa, whoa, whoa. You'll have to pick someone else to be your best friend, May," he said. "Lucille is *my* best friend these days. Remember?"

May stood there a second. Then she leaned into Sheldon's face.

"You're not *fooling* anyone, Mr. Potts. You're just *pretending* to like Lucille, the

same as I am," she said. "You're just trying
to get her to tell you where the golden egg
is."

Lucille looked shocked at that comment.

"That's not true! Is it, Sheldon? You're not just *pretending* to like me, right?" she asked. "'Cause I told you before . . . I don't know where the golden egg is. My daddy hid it all by himself. And he wouldn't let me peek."

She glanced at her daddy very annoyed.

"I *tried* to make him tell me where he hid it, Shelsie. But Daddy locked his lips. And he threw away the key."

Sheldon clenched his fists.

"Drat! The old invisible-key trick," he said. "I hate that one!"

Finally, he took a breath and calmed himself down.

Then he patted Lucille very sweet.

"Don't worry, my springy little lamb," he said. "I will *still* find the golden egg and win the playdate. I'm positive I will."

He lowered his voice kind of private.

"I'm wearing a lucky charm today," he said real soft.

Lucille's mouth came open at that news.

"A lucky charm?" she shouted. "You have a lucky charm? What is it, Shelsie? What is it?"

Sheldon pointed down at his shirt.

"See that little egg dribble on my collar right there?" he asked. "That little egg dribble ran off my chin at breakfast. And look, Lucille . . . it landed on my collar, in the exact shape of—"

He paused real dramatic.

". . . an *egg*," he whispered.

Lucille did a shiver.

"Ooooh, *Shelsie*! That seems like magic, almost," she said.

Sheldon nodded.

"I know it, Lucille. It seems *exactly* like magic, almost," he said. "My grampa Ned has had every shirt stain in the book. And he said that when egg dribble lands in the shape of an egg, it means—"

Sheldon swallowed hard.

". . . *may the egg be with me.*"

Lucille did another shiver.

Sheldon smiled.

"With a magic-egg shirt like this, I can't lose today, Lucille," he said. "I just *can't.*"

After that, he hurried over to the nanna. And he tried to show her his egg shirt. But the nanna backed up from him.

Then she quick grabbed Lucille's daddy. And she said the words, *Do something!*

The daddy cleared his loud throat.

"Boys and girls. May I please have your attention?" he said. "First, I would like to welcome you all to the party today."

Lucille hopped in front of him.

"Yes! Yes! Welcome to my party! And welcome to my giant house. And welcome to my big, huge yard, too!"

She bent down and touched the grass.

"See how perfect the lawn is cut, everyone?" she said. "That's because we have a real professional gardener. On account of rich people don't know the first thing about yard work. Right, Daddy? Plus rich people don't like to get our hands dirty."

Everyone looked at the daddy's hands.

He quick put them in his pockets.

Lucille kept on talking.

"And did everyone see my brand-new, expensive Easter dress?" she asked.

She spun around and flounced herself.

"This dress is made out of fancy, floaty

chiffon. And fancy, floaty chiffon is as light as a feather," she said.

She fluffed her flouncy skirt.

"Who would like me to hop in the air and make it float? Please clap your hands," she said.

But before we could clap, Lucille already started hopping.

She hopped and hopped until sweaty came on her lip.

Then Lucille's mother quick ran over. And she dabbed her face with a tissue.

I looked at Herbert.

"This family has some serious perspiration issues, I believe," I said.

Just then, Lucille's daddy cleared his loud throat again.

"Children, as all of you know, we're going to be having a picnic and an Easter-egg hunt today. But for this party to go smoothly, we're going to need your complete cooperation. Okay?" he asked.

"OKAY!" we shouted back. "OKAY! OKAY!"

The daddy smiled.

"The first thing I'd like you to do is get into a nice straight line," he said.

"A NICE STRAIGHT LINE! A NICE STRAIGHT LINE!" we shouted again.

Room One is excellent at repeating things.

The daddy looked at us.

"Okay. Fine. As I was saying, if you get into a nice straight line, we'll lead you to the picnic grounds in the back of the house."

"THE BACK OF THE HOUSE! THE BACK OF THE HOUSE!" we hollered out.

The daddy stopped smiling.

We were starting to get on his nerves, I think.

Next to him, Lucille's mother and nanna were doing deep breathing.

The brother had already gone inside to watch TV.

Finally, all of us got in a nice straight line.

Then the mother and daddy and nanna did a group hug with each other.

And they led us to the picnic grounds.

AND WOWIE WOW WOW!

I could not believe my eyeballs!

'Cause on the way, we passed Lucille's hugie big swimming pool! And it was inside a big glass house!

All of Room One did a gasp at that sight!

I ran to Lucille and hugged her around the middle.

"Lucille! Lucille! You are even richer than you used to be! Your swimming pool is in a big glass house now! And so my play-date with you will be even funner than I thought!"

Lucille took my hands off her.

"Silly Junie B. Jones. You know the rules. If you want the playdate, you're going to have to find the golden egg. And that's not going to be easy. Because my boyfriend Shelsie is wearing his magic-egg shirt," she said.

She looked at Sheldon and did a wink.

Sheldon winked back.

May was watching that action.

"Hey, hey, hey!" she grouched. "That better not be a secret wink about the golden egg. 'Cause if you're winking about the golden egg, I'm telling!"

She poked Sheldon with her finger.

"I'm going to be watching every move you make, Sheldon Potts," she said. "I'm going to be all over you like a cheap suit."

I did a frown at that comment.

I do not know what *a cheap suit* means, exactly.

But here is what I *do* know.

For the first time in my life, May was right, I think.

Whoever wanted to find the golden egg could *not* let Sheldon out of their sight.

5

■ ■ ■ ■ ■ ■ ■ ■ ■ ■

The Jelly Bean Game

Lucille's daddy clapped his loud hands together.

"Boys and girls, please find a seat at one of the picnic tables. Lunch will be served shortly," he called.

I waited to see where Sheldon was going to sit.

May waited, too.

'Cause both of us had to keep track of that guy, of course.

Only too bad for me.

Because as soon as Sheldon picked a

table, Lucille sat down next to him.

And *VAROOM!*

May slid in on his *other* side.

And I got shut out!

"Wait! Hold it! No fair!" I said.

Then I quick tried to squeeze myself between May and Sheldon. But May would not budge herself.

I did a *grr* face at her.

May hissed like a snake.

I stood there very puzzled.

I do not actually have a comeback for a hiss.

Finally, I went to the other side of the table. And I sat down across from them.

"That dumb May," I grumped to just myself. "She keeps getting one step ahead of me today. Plus Sheldon is one step ahead of me, too."

I looked across the table.

Lucille was whispering to Sheldon very secret.

May leaned her head over. And she listened through Sheldon's other ear.

Whispers can come right through Sheldon's head, apparently.

I put my chin in my hands.

"I don't stand a *chance* in this stupid egg hunt," I said to Herb.

He gave me a little pat.

Sometimes a little pat is all a friend can do.

Only guess what?

Just then, something very nice happened!

And it's called, *Lucille's nanna walked over to where I was sitting. And she sat in a chair at the end of my table!*

I jumped up real thrilled.

"NANNA! NANNA! LOOK! LOOK!

IT'S ME! IT'S JUNIE B. JONES! AND YOU ARE SITTING RIGHT EXACTLY NEXT TO ME!" I shouted.

The nanna glanced her eyes at Lucille's mother and daddy.

"Yes. I know, dear. I lost the coin toss," she said kind of annoyed.

I sat back down and tickled her arm.

"This reminds me of when we ate dinner together last year," I said. "That was very fun. Except I accidentally broke your crystal glass. Remember that, Nanna? Huh? Do you?"

The nanna nodded.

"Oh yes. I remember," she said.

I thought back. "Plus I accidentally busted your feather pillow. And if I'm not mistaken, I spilled beanie weenies on your expensive linen tablecloth," I said.

The nanna looked at me.

"You're not mistaken," she said back.

I smiled and patted her hand.

"Good times," I said real soft.

May heard me talking.

"Well, Lucille and I are going to have good times, too. Right, Lucille? When I come to swim in your pool, that will *really* be good times," she said.

Sheldon looked at her and grinned.

"Don't count your chickens before they're hashed, May," he said.

The nanna did a little chuckle.

"I think you mean *hatched,* dear. It's don't count your chickens before they're *hatched.* Not *hashed,*" she said.

Sheldon raised his eyebrows.

"Really? Are you *sure*? 'Cause at our house, my aunt Bunny brings chicken hash for dinner every Sunday," he said. "Chicken hash is her specialty."

He smiled real proud.

"Aunt Bunny was a chef in prison," he said.

The nanna's face went funny.

She lowered her head to the table. And she rested her cheek on her napkin.

I leaned my face down next to her.

"Speaking of bunnies . . . Lucille said the Easter Bunny would be here today. Only I haven't actually seen him yet. And so where is he, anyway, Nanna?" I asked.

Lucille did a huff at me.

"Nosy Junie B. Jones. Why did you have to ask that question?" she said. "My nanna does not want to talk about that. Do you, Nanna? You made a teensy little mistake about the bunny. And you don't want anyone to know about how you almost ruined the party."

The nanna did a groan.

Lucille kept on talking.

"My nanna was in charge of hiring the Easter Bunny. Only instead of hiring the *real* Easter Bunny, she hired a cheap, *fake* Easter Bunny. Right, Nanna?"

The nanna did not reply.

Lucille went on.

"The fake bunny came to our house to get his pay yesterday. Only his fur was real matty. And the top of his ear was chewed off. But he told my nanna that he *freshened up* nicely. And so Nanna gave him cash money in advance. And then he hopped out the front door. And he never came back."

The nanna raised her head. "Thank you,

Lucille," she said. "Thank you for sharing that with everyone."

"You're welcome, Nanna," said Lucille very pleasant. "You're welcome."

The nanna rolled her eyes.

Lucille does not understand sarcastic, I believe.

Just then, Lucille's daddy stood up at his picnic table. And he said it was time "to get this show on the road."

He held up a silver bell and rang it in the air.

TING-A-LING-A-LING!

TING-A-LING-A-LING!

Then boom!

Waiters started bringing food from all over the place.

And it was the deliciousest food I ever saw!

There were barbecued hamburgers! And

tasty hot dogs! And crispy chicken fingers! And crunchy salad! And yummy potato chips! And sweetish pickles! Plus there were even delicious devilish eggs!

"Whoa! What a spread!" I said.

I stuffed a devilish egg in my mouth. Also I stuffed in a pickle. And some chips! And a giant chicken finger!

I didn't stop stuffing for a real long time.

Then finally, I leaned back. And I rubbed my big fat tummy.

"Whew! I am about to bust a gusset!" I said. "Are you, Nanna? Huh? Are you about to bust a gusset, too?"

The nanna frowned her eyebrows. "Ladies don't bust *gussets*, Junie B.," she said.

I was surprised to hear that information.

"Really?" I said. "Then what do ladies bust?"

Roger raised his hand.

"At our house, we bust our guts," he said.

Herb smiled.

"At our house, we bust our buttons," he said.

Sheldon stood up.

"At our house, we just unzip our pants," he said.

After that, everyone at our table laughed and laughed.

Except for not the nanna.

Finally, all of us got finished eating. And the waiters took our plates away.

Then wowie wow wow!

Lucille's daddy brought out the most beautiful box I ever saw!

It was wrapped in shiny yellow paper with twirly, curly ribbons!

He held it way high in the air so all of us could see.

"Whoa! Whose birthday is it?" I shouted real excited.

Lucille jumped up and giggled.

"That's not a *birthday* present, Junie B. It's a *game* prize!" she said. "Before we hunt for eggs, we're going to play a very fun game. And whoever wins that prize will get the thrill of a lifetime! Right, Daddy?"

The daddy smiled.

"Well, we certainly *hope* the winner will be thrilled," he said. "It's a pretty good prize, we think."

Just then, he put down the box. And he pulled a big jar of jelly beans out of a paper bag.

"This game is called the Jelly Bean Game," he said. "Can everyone see all the jelly beans in the jar? We've got lots of colors, don't we? We've got reds and yellows and blues and blacks and greens and oranges and whites."

He stopped and held up his finger.

"*But,*" he said, "in this whole big jar of jelly beans, there is just one *purple* one."

All of us made a hushy sound.

"OOOOH," we said together. "JUST ONE PURPLE ONE."

The daddy smiled.

Then he put the jar back in the bag so we couldn't see the colors anymore.

"Okay. Now I'm going to walk around to each picnic table. And each of you will have a chance to reach in the jar and pull out a jelly bean," he said. "But remember. You may only pull out *one*, okay?"

"OKAY!" we hollered. "OKAY! OKAY!"

Lucille hurried over and held up the beautiful box.

"And remember this, too! The first person to pull out the *purple* jelly bean will get this prize!" she said. "The thrill of a lifetime!"

All of us clapped and clapped.

Then we bounced and giggled and wiggled and clapped. And we waited for the jelly-bean jar to come to us.

It was the nervousest wait of my life, I think. Because what if someone got the purple jelly bean before I even got my turn? That would ruin my whole entire chance!

I put my hands in front of my eyes.

Then I peeked through my fingers.

And I watched the children pick.

Roger's table went first.

He picked a red bean.

Then Camille picked an orange bean.

And Chenille picked a green bean.

And Shirley picked a blue bean.

My table came next.

My heart beat faster.

José picked a yellow bean.

Then Lennie picked a white bean. And May picked *another* white bean. And Sheldon picked a black bean.

And then at last! At last!

It was time for *me*!

My heart was pounding like crazy.

I bent over and did some deep breathing.

The daddy held out the bag to me.

I breathed some more.

"Okay, Junie B.," he said. "Anytime now."

I stood up and did a gulp.

Then, very slow, I reached my hand inside

the bag. And I felt all around for purple.

I wrinkled my eyebrows real curious.

"Hmm. What does purple feel like, I wonder?" I said to just myself.

The daddy said *please hurry up*.

I swished my fingers through the jar some more.

Then, all of a sudden, I *felt* it, I tell you!

I felt *purple*!

It felt roundish . . . and beanish . . . and purplish!

I grabbed it real tight.

Then I quick pulled my hand out of the jar.

And I opened up my fingers.

AND GUESS WHAT?

GUESS WHAT?

GUESS WHAT?

6

■ ■ ■ ■ ■ ■ ■ ■ ■

Me and Santa

IT WAS PURPLE!

THAT'S WHAT!

I jumped up and down and all around.

"Purple! Purple! I got purple!" I shouted. "I'm getting the thrill of a lifetime! I'm getting the thrill of a lifetime!"

I skipped over to May. And I smiled real big in her face.

Then I skipped to the middle of the tables. And I did a giant bow.

Giant bows are very enjoyable. Even when no one is actually clapping for you.

After I stopped bowing, Lucille's daddy handed me the beautiful box.

I pulled off the paper as fast as I could.

Then I lifted off its lid.

And I stared inside.

"Hmm," I said very puzzled. "It's, um . . . a box of pink fur."

I scratched my head.

"I've always wanted a box of pink fur . . . possibly," I said.

Lucille laughed real loud.

"Silly Junie B. Jones! It's not *just* a box of pink fur! Take it out so you can see what it *really* is!" she said.

Then—just as I was about to pick it up—Lucille grabbed the pink fur.

And she held it up in front of me.

And that is the last actual fun I had at the party.

"A bunny suit! See? It's a bunny suit," shouted Lucille. "Junie B. is going to be our party's very own Easter Bunny!"

May laughed real loud.

"SHE'S GOING TO BE OUR *DUMB* BUNNY, YOU MEAN!" she called out. "JUNIE JONES IS GOING TO BE OUR VERY OWN DUMB BUNNY!"

Just then, the rest of the children began to laugh, too.

Lucille stamped her mad foot at them.

"Stop it!" she said. "Junie B. is not going to be our dumb bunny! She's going to be our Easter Bunny! This is the finest bunny costume money can buy."

She held it out to me.

"Here, Junie B. Put it on and show everyone how cute it is!"

She handed me the costume.

I swallowed real hard.

"Yeah, only here's the problem, Lucille. I don't actually like costumes that much. Not even at Halloween," I said. "Mostly, I just like dressing up as Junie B. Jones, and that's all."

Lucille's whole mouth came open at that news.

She put her hands over her ears.

"Oh no! Do NOT tell me that, Junie B. Jones!" she said. "You *have* to be the bunny. You *have* to!"

She ran to her daddy and pulled on his arm.

"*Make* her, Daddy! Make Junie B. be the bunny! *Make* her!" she yelled.

Lucille's daddy rubbed his chin.

"Well, we certainly would like it if Junie B. was the bunny," he said. "But we can't really *make* her, Lucille."

Lucille jumped up and down at me.

"You're going to ruin my whole party,

Junie B. Jones!" she grouched. "We hired an expensive photographer and everything! We're all supposed to get our pictures taken with you!"

My ears perked up at that news.

"Pictures?" I said kind of curious.

Lucille nodded.

"Yes! Pictures!" she said back. "The photographer has a seat set up for you in the flower garden!"

My ears perked up some more.

"A seat?" I said. "You mean like . . . a *Santa* seat?"

Lucille jumped way high in the air.

"Yes, yes! Exactly like a Santa seat!" she said. "The photographer is waiting for you! You're going to be a celebrity, Junie B.! Will you do it? Huh? Will you?"

I sat down in the grass to think about it.

Lucille's daddy bent down next to me.

"You don't have to do this if you don't want to, Junie B.," he said. "But we do need to get on with the party. So could you make up your mind, please? Do you want to be the bunny? Or do you want us to get someone else?"

Just then, Sheldon shot his hand in the air.

"I'll do it! I'll do it!" he yelled real excited. "I would love to have my picture taken with everyone!"

"Me too!" hollered Shirley. "I would love to do that, too!"

I looked at those two kind of curious.

Maybe I was wrong about this situation.

Maybe being a famous bunny really *was* the thrill of a lifetime.

I pulled the bunny suit closer to me.

Then, very slow, I put one foot inside the costume . . . then the other foot . . .

Then *ZIP, ZIP, SNAP!*

The daddy fastened me up!

And bingo!

I was a bunny.

7

Polite Rules

I looked down at myself.

My bunny feet were bigger than clown feet.

Also, my ears were floppish.

And my bunny hands looked like giant paw mitts.

I held them out in front of me.

"I could take a pie out of the oven with these things," I said.

Lucille skipped around me and clapped.

"Yay! Yay! Yay! We have a bunny! We have a bunny!" she sang real happy.

After that, she grabbed my bunny paw.
And she started skipping me to the flower
garden.

Only too bad for me. 'Cause skipping
with giant bunny feet does not actually
work that good.

And so . . . *KERPLOP!*

I fell right over in the grass.

Some of the children started to laugh.

Lucille shooed them away.

Then she quick hurried to pick me up. Only her dress started to get wrinkly. And so she dropped me in the grass again. And she smoothed her skirt very neat. Plus also she fluffed her hair. And she shined her shoes.

After that, she yelled to her daddy real urgent.

"DADDY! DADDY! THE BUNNY'S DOWN! COME GET THE BUNNY! COME GET THE BUNNY!"

The daddy ran over and picked me up.

Then he started carrying me to the flower garden.

It felt embarrassing up there.

I tapped on his head.

"This does not actually make me feel like a celebrity," I said.

The daddy kept on going.

I tapped on his head again.

"No one actually carries Santa," I said.

Just then, we got to the flower garden.

The daddy put me down. And he showed me the photographer.

His name was Bud.

Bud sat me in my bunny seat. And he arranged my floppy ears.

After that, he went to his camera. And he took my picture.

"Beautiful!" he said. "Gorgeous!"

I smiled.

I liked this Bud.

Pretty soon, the children lined up to get their pictures taken with me.

And guess what?

My bestest friend named Herbert was the very first one in line!

He zoomed to my seat real happy.

"I think you look nice in that bunny costume," he said. "You don't even look stupid, hardly."

I smiled again.

"Thank you, Herbert. You don't look stupid, too," I said back.

After that, both of us said *cheese*. And Bud took our picture.

Lennie came next.

Then after Lennie came José. And after José came Shirley. And after Shirley came all of the other children in Room One.

Except for not May.

Instead, May sat in the grass all by herself. Because *she* was not a celebrity, of course.

I said *cheese* a million times.

Bud kept on saying *beautiful* and *gorgeous* to me.

I felt very puffery inside.

"I am an excellent celebrity," I told him. "I am making these children's day."

Bud laughed.

I do not know why.

Finally, all the pictures got taken.

Bud shook my paw mitt goodbye.

I will miss him.

After that, Herb and I walked back to the picnic grounds.

And wait till you hear this!

Lucille's mother was passing out baskets for the egg hunt!

I started to run to get my basket.

Only what do you know?

KERPLOP!

I tripped and fell in the grass again.

The children laughed some more.

I pretended I didn't care.

"It's fun to fall," I said real stupid.

Even Herb rolled his eyes at that one.

Lucille's mother helped me up and gave me a basket.

I looked at her very upset.

"Yeah, only how am I supposed to hunt for eggs in these big, giant bunny feet?" I said. "I can't even run in these clumsy things. Plus also, I can't tackle or scuffle."

The mother looked shocked at me.

"Tackle?" she said. *"Scuffle?* Oh my, no. This is going to be a *polite* egg hunt, Junie B. There will be no running, or tackling, or scuffling. We're all going to behave like little ladies and gentlemen."

Just then, there was a loud commotion behind me.

I turned around.

May was pointing and yelling at Sheldon and Lucille.

"Stop whispering secrets, Lucille!" she shouted. "You're telling Sheldon where the golden egg is! I *know* you are! I'm telling your daddy! I'm telling your daddy!"

The daddy rushed over there and separated those guys.

"This bickering has *got* to stop!" he said.

"If you three can't behave yourselves, you won't be hunting for eggs at all."

I smiled at that comment.

That would be a nice development, I thought.

After he finished scolding them, Lucille's daddy blew a whistle. And he told us to line up at the starting line.

Everyone zoomed past me.

I lifted my feet and stepped real careful.

Then, finally, I got there. And the daddy started telling us the egg-hunt rules.

"Rule number one," he said. "No running.

"Rule number two: No pushing, pulling, or grabbing.

"Rule number three: No trampling the flowers and plants.

"And finally, rule number four: Do not go anywhere that is roped off."

He looked up and down the line at us.

"Does everyone understand the rules?" he asked.

I thought for a minute.

Then I raised my hand.

"Also, there is no tackling or scuffling, correct?" I said. "'Cause I have already been informed about that situation."

The daddy looked odd at me.

"Well, of course there's no tackling or scuffling, Junie B.," he said. "That goes without saying."

I thought some more.

Then I pointed at my giant bunny feet.

"Plus there should be no tripping the bunny, right?" I asked. "'Cause the bunny is wearing unfair feet."

The daddy frowned. "There's no tripping *anyone,* Junie B.," he said.

I nodded.

"Yes, but there's *especially* no tripping the bunny, correct?" I asked again.

The daddy sucked in his cheeks.

"Okay, fine. There's *especially* no tripping the bunny," he said. "Now, may I continue?"

I smiled.

The daddy continued.

"The hunt will begin when I count to three," he said. "You will have thirty minutes to hunt for the eggs. When I blow my whistle, you will all stop hunting immediately. And you will bring your baskets back to the table."

Roger raised his hand.

"What's the prize for finding the most eggs?" he asked.

Lucille's mother smiled.

Then she held up a big wad of flowers.

"The person who has the most eggs will receive this beautiful bouquet for his or her mother," she said. "They're irises from our flower garden. I picked them myself. Aren't they lovely?"

Roger looked at the irises.

"I think my mother would rather have a set of Power Rangers," he said.

Lucille's mother made squinty eyes at him.

That meant no Power Rangers, I believe.

Just then, the daddy blew his whistle.

"Okay! Is everyone ready to start?" he hollered.

"READY!" we hollered back. "READY, READY, READY!"

And so the daddy raised his hand in the air.

And—
"ONE . . . TWO . . . THREE!"
The egg hunt was started!

8

Swooping

The children *ran*!

They ran *everywhere*, I tell you!

They ran to and fro! And up and down! And back and forth! And here and there!

Also, Roger ran sideways.

And Lennie ran in a circle.

I watched them very fascinated.

Some of the children were tackling and scuffling.

Sheldon went through a shrub.

That's when Lucille's daddy blew his whistle again.

TWEET! TWEET! TWEET!

"Everyone come back here right now!" he shouted real mad.

Everyone came back.

Sheldon had a stick in his ear.

He sputtered and stuttered and pointed at May.

"She *pushed* me! She pushed me! May pushed me through a bush!"

May stamped her foot.

"No, I did *not*, Sheldon! I did not push you! You pushed yourself!" she said.

She turned and looked at the daddy.

"It was the darnedest thing you ever saw," she said. "He shoved himself right through that shrub."

The daddy stood there a real long time.

Then he walked to a picnic bench.

And he sat down real slow.

And he hit himself in the head.

I went over and tapped on him.

"I would just like to point out that the bunny did not run," I said. "The bunny was the only one who walked."

May overheard me.

"That's because the bunny *can't* run or the bunny falls down," she called. "The bunny should *not* get credit for that!"

The daddy hit himself in the head again.

I walked back to Herbert.

He looked kind of worried.

"The daddy is coming unglued," he said.

I nodded.

"Yes," I said. "The daddy is going to need backup, I believe."

Backup is the grown-up word for *the police might need to come, possibly.*

And guess what? Me and Herb were not

the only ones thinking that, either.

'Cause just then, Lucille's nanna hollered out real loud.

"*Enough!*" she hollered. "I have had enough of this nonsense with you children!"

Then she cupped her hands around her mouth. And she shouted out a brand-new rule.

It was called, *If there's any more running or fighting, she is going to call the cops.*

All of the children did a loud gulp.

I looked at Herbert.

"That new rule seems a little harsh," I said.

Only guess what else?

The new rule worked, I think.

'Cause pretty soon, the nanna started the egg hunt again.

And *this* time, no one ran at all!

No one even *walked*, hardly.

Instead, we all behaved like little ladies and gentlemen. And we hunted for eggs very polite.

May stuck to Sheldon like glue.

I tried to stick to him, too. But my giant feet could not keep up that good.

May kept on grouching.

"You're not going to get the golden egg before I do, Sheldon. Even if you know where it is, I'll still beat you to it," she said. "I'm all over you like flies on egg salad."

Sheldon rolled his eyes.

"But I don't *know* where the golden egg is, May," he said. "I've already told you that. I don't know *anything* at all."

I cupped my mitts around my mouth.

"*I* believe you, Sheldon! *I* believe you don't know anything at all!" I shouted.

"I've *never* thought you've known anything at all!"

After that, I hurried to catch up to him.

'Cause I definitely thought he knew something, of course.

Sheldon turned to wait for me.

Then, all of a sudden, he glanced down at the ground. And he did a loud gasp.

"I SEE ONE! I SEE ONE! I SEE ONE!" he shouted.

May and I turned to look.

There was a bright green egg under the bushes.

Sheldon clapped and laughed.

Then he hurried over to pick it up.

But . . .

WHOOSH!

SWOOP!

SCOOP!

May ducked underneath him speedy fast. And *she* picked it up instead!

"I GOT IT! I GOT IT! I GOT IT!" she screeched.

Then she put the egg in her basket and danced all around.

Sheldon's face got sputtery mad.

But—before he could even yell at her— he did another gasp.

"I SEE ONE! I SEE ONE! I SEE ONE!" he shouted, even louder than before.

Then he clapped his hands.

And he laughed real happy.

And he hurried over to pick it up.

But . . .

WHOOSH!

SWOOP!

SCOOP!

May beat him to it *again*!

"TWO! TWO! NOW I HAVE TWO!"
she hollered.

She jumped in the air and kicked her
feet.

"I swooped! I'm a swooper! I swoop!"
she said.

She ran back to Sheldon and leaned in
his face.

"I *knew* I would beat you at this game,"
she said. "Now I have *two* eggs, and you
and Junie B. have . . ."

She leaned her head into our baskets.

"Hmm. Let's count them . . . ZERO!
Ha! You have zero. And I have two! Two to
zero. Two to zippedy-zip zero!"

Sheldon looked at me real upset.

I frowned my eyes at him.

"Helpful hint," I said. "Stop shouting, *'I
SEE ONE.'*"

Sheldon pointed at his magic-egg shirt.

"But I just don't *get* it, Junie B.," he said. "My grampa said that *the egg is with me.* So why isn't this magic shirt working?"

I looked closer at the egg dribble.

"Maybe it's not lucky," I said. "Maybe it's just dirty."

Sheldon slumped his shoulders.

Then he reached down his finger. And he flicked off the egg.

Only wait till you hear this!

Just as he flicked it, his eyes got big and wide again.

This time, I hurried to cover his mouth with my hand.

But Sheldon shouted right through my paw mitt.

"I SEE ONE! I SEE ONE! I SEE ONE!" he shouted.

Then, before he could even move his feet . . .

WHOOSH!

SWOOP!

SCOOP!

May grabbed egg number *three*!

She twirled in a happy circle around us.

"THREE TO ZERO! THREE TO ZERO! IT'S THREE TO ZERO!" she yelled.

Sheldon stood real still.

Then, very slow, he put down his basket.

And he stretched out the sides of his mouth with his fingers.

And he stuck his tongue out at May.

That was appropriate behavior, I believe.

After that, he snatched his basket up again. And he tried to rush away from May.

But too bad for Sheldon.

Because May stayed right exactly on his heels.

They were walking too fast for me to keep up.

I stopped and watched them go.

Then I did a big sigh.

And I walked to a tree stump.

And I sat down very glum.

"I hate being this dumb bunny," I said. "'Cause my feet are too big. And my legs are too slow. And my paw mitts are way too clumsy."

I slumped my shoulders and looked in the empty basket.

I did another sigh.

'Cause let's face it.

The bunny was a rotten egg.

9

■ ■ ■ ■ ■ ■ ■ ■ ■ ■

Lucky Bunny!

Sheldon found three more eggs.

May swooped all of them.

Every time she swooped, she shouted her head off.

"FOUR! FOUR! NOW I HAVE FOUR!"

"FIVE! FIVE! NOW I HAVE FIVE!"

"SIX! SIX! I JUST GOT SIX!"

Six was Sheldon's limit, apparently.

He stomped to my tree stump and threw his empty basket in the grass.

"That's it! I'm done! I'm not looking for one more egg for that girl. Let her find her own stupid eggs! I quit!" he said.

May came chasing after him.

"No, Sheldon! No! You can't quit! You *can't*! Come on! We're a *team*!" she said. "We're . . . we're *Team May*!"

Sheldon did a huffy breath at her.

"No, we're *not*. We're *not* Team *May*," he grouched. "I'm an egg finder. And you're some creepy swooping bird girl who steals them."

May's mouth opened real shocked.

"I did *not* steal your eggs, Sheldon Potts! Those eggs were still in the grass when I picked them up! Just because you *saw* them first didn't make them *yours*!" she said. "*Picking them up* is what makes eggs yours."

Sheldon started to yell back.

Then he stopped and looked at me.

"Shoot," he said. "I think she has a valid point there."

May smiled real smuggy.

"Thank you, Sheldon," she said.

"You're *not* welcome," he said back. "And I'm *still* not looking for any more eggs, May. I'm still quitting."

May was not expecting that development.

She started to sputter.

"But . . . but you *have* to look for more eggs, Sheldon! You have to! Just a couple more eggs and I can win this whole thing," she said. "Plus you still haven't found the golden egg for me yet!"

Just then, the nanna walked by.

May reached out and grabbed her arm.

"Tell him, Nanna! Tell him he can't quit!" she said. "Sheldon is on my team!

And when you're on a team, you *can't* quit! It's not fair!"

The nanna looked puzzled for a second.

Then she did a little frown and shook her head.

"Oh my. No," she said. "I'm sorry, dear. But there are no *teams* on an egg hunt. An egg hunt is an *individual* competition."

May did not like that answer.

She pulled on the nanna's arm some more.

"But . . . but . . . Sheldon *has* to help me! He *has* to! He—"

The nanna interrupted her.

"If you don't let go of my arm, I'm going to give you a swat, dear," she said.

May quick let go.

The nanna smoothed herself and walked on.

Sheldon laughed real loud.

"I like that nanna," he said.

I smiled.

"I like that nanna, too," I said.

I nudged him with my elbow.

"Maybe someday she will be your nanna-in-law."

Sheldon did a loud hoot.

After that, we did a high five, and a low five, and a medium five. Then I scooted over so he could share my tree stump.

Lucille spotted us there.

Her whole face lighted up when she saw Sheldon.

"Shelsie! Shelsie! I've been looking for you! Where's your basket?" she asked. "Did you find the golden egg yet? Huh? Did you, Shelsie? Did you?"

Sheldon's face went funny.

"Um, well . . . my magic-egg shirt didn't work out that good, Lucille," he said. "I kept finding the eggs. But May kept swooping them. And so now I'm just sort of . . . well, you know . . ."

May butted her head in.

"QUITTING!" she hollered. "He's quitting, Lucille! Tell him he can't quit! Tell him right now!"

Lucille raised her eyebrows.

"You're *quitting*, Shelsie? Why are you quitting? You have to find the golden egg, remember?" she said. "If you don't find the golden egg, I will have to swim in my pool with someone I don't actually care for."

She started to get annoyed.

"Think of *me*, Sheldon! You have to think of *me*!" she said. "Don't you know anything about being a boyfriend? Boyfriends do *not* let their girlfriends swim with people they don't care for!"

Sheldon didn't answer.

Lucille's face got madder.

Sweat came on her head and lip.

"Well, for goodness' sake! Don't just sit there, Sheldon! Go find that egg!" she snapped.

Then she wiped her sweat on her expensive dress sleeve. And she stomped away.

Sheldon watched her go.

Finally he turned and looked at me.

"My little lamb did not actually handle that well," he said kind of quiet.

He paused a second.

"Also, she turned into a sweaty dripball," he added.

Just then, May stuck her head in between us.

"Come on, Sheldon! You heard what Lucille told you!" she said. "You have to find the golden egg! Come on! Find it right now!"

Then she grabbed his arm and tried to pull him up. But Sheldon did not budge himself.

He shook her off like she was a bug.

I admire that style.

After that, both of us sat there until the hunt was almost over. And then we started walking back to the picnic tables.

Only too bad for me.

Because I forgot to pick up my hugie big feet. And I fell down in the grass again.

And *that's* when it happened!

I saw something *gleamy*!

It was gleaming right in my eyes, I mean!

I blinked and looked again.

Then I quick tried to cover my mouth with my paw mitt.

But the words came rushing right out of my lips.

"THE GOLDEN EGG! THE GOLDEN EGG! I SEE THE GOLDEN EGG!"

May and Sheldon looked down and saw it, too.

For a second, all of us stood there real frozen.

And then . . .

OOMPHFF!

FOOMFF!

PHIFFOOPHFF!

We all dived for it at once!

And . . .

SLAP!

SLAP!

SLAP!

We piled our hands on top!

"I'VE GOT IT!"

"I'VE GOT IT!"

"I'VE GOT IT!" we shouted.

Then suddenly, all of us got very silent. And we stared and stared at our hand pile.

My heart started to pound.

I stared some more.

Then my mouth fell open. And I did a loud gasp.

BECAUSE THE EGG WAS UNDER *MY* GIANT PAW MITT, THAT'S WHY!

"OH MY GOSH! I really *do* got it!" I hollered.

Sheldon frowned.

"Are you sure?" he asked.

He wiggled his fingers to locate himself.

"Shoot," he said. "I was hoping that big paw was mine."

I looked odd at him.

That was a joke, I hope.

"Well, at least you beat May," I said real happy. "Beating May is still good, Sheldon."

Then, *KABOOM!*

May exploded like a firecracker!

She yanked her hand off the top of the pile. And she slapped it on the ground.

"HE DID *NOT* BEAT ME, JUNIE JONES! Sheldon has *zero* eggs and I have six! How can you say he beat me, you big dumb bunny?" she yelled.

That's when I exploded, too.

"I AM *NOT* A DUMB BUNNY, MAY!" I shouted back. "I am the celebrity of this whole entire occasion! Plus you didn't even find one single egg on your own! And so I will *show* you how Sheldon can beat you! I will show you right exactly now, in fact!"

Then—without even thinking about it—I quick slid my paw mitt off of the golden egg! And I let Sheldon's hand drop on top!

"*THERE!* HA! SEE, MAY? SEE? Now *Sheldon* has the golden egg! And you don't! And the golden egg is the winner of this whole event!" I said.

May's eyes got as big as bowls.

Sheldon's eyes got big, too.

He grabbed the egg in both his hands. And he jumped up like a rocket.

May slumped her face in the grass.

Then *TWEET! TWEET! TWEET!*

The nanna blew the whistle.

And that was that.

The egg hunt was over.

10

Decisions

Monday

Dear first-grade journal,
 Today at school Sheldon keeps on hugging me.
 Lucille keeps hugging me, too.
 May keeps glaring at me.
 She needs anger-management classes, I believe.

I quit writing and thought about the party.

May didn't win the most eggs.

'Cause guess who did!

My friend José, that's who!

And guess who got to present the flowers to him?

Me!

The bunny!

José was the happiest boy I ever saw.

He jumped way high in the air.

"Las flores para mi madre! Las flores para mi madre!" he said. "Muchas gracias, conejito!"

I giggled very happy.

Conejito means "bunny" in Spanish, I think.

I smiled at that memory.

Then I started to write in my journal some more.

Sometimes I'm not happy about giving the golden egg to Sheldon.

'Cause I made that decision ~~desishun~~ on the spurt of the moment. And I still want to swim in Lucille's hot water.

Only here is the confusing ~~confuzing~~ thing.

Sometimes I am happy about what I did for Sheldon.

'Cause seeing his face made me smile inside.

And so that is something for me to think about, I guess.

And guess what else?

I am not calling May dumb
bunny anymore, probably.
'Cause bunnies aren't that
dumb, of course. And so now
I am going to call May a
different name.
Uh-oh . . .
She just glared at me again.
I think I will offer her a
jelly bean.
'Cause that would be a nice
gesture by me.
Please stand by . . .

I put down my pencil and reached into my
pocket.

Then I pulled out the candy bag I brought to school. And I held it out to her.

"Would you like a jelly bean, Bird Girl?" I said real pleasant.

May sputtered and stuttered very shocked.

Then she quick raised her hand to tattle.

"MR. SCARY! MR. SCARY! MR. SCARY!" she hollered.

Mr. Scary looked back at us.

His face did not look delightful.

I ducked down my head.

May did a gulp.

Then she lowered her hand and started counting to twenty.

No action was taken.

I smiled very relieved.

Then finally, I picked up my pencil one more time. And I finished my journal page.

May does not like her new name, apparently.

That is going to work out just fine, I think.

Have a ~~happy~~ HOPPY day!

Your friend,

Junie B, Smart Bunny